Published by Kelly Franco

Ordering Information:

For details, contact www.kelly-franco.com

First Edition

ISBN 9780997506105

First Printing 2016

A Tail of Two Friends

by Kelly Franco

Illustrated by Alexandria Gold

It was Thursday afternoon and 6-year-old Olive had just stepped off the school bus in front of her house.

"Hey Mom!" she said. "And hello Lulu!" she exclaimed as she ran over to her dog and gave her the biggest hug.

"Olive, honey, your father and I have something to tell you. Can you sit down on the couch, please?" her mother asked.

"Olive," her father began, "I got offered a new job at work, which I'm very excited about. And the best part is we'll be moving to a completely different state!"

Olive's mouth fell open and her eyes grew wide with fear. "The best part? No, this is terrible! What about my friends?"

"Well," her mother said, "you can still keep in touch with them and you'll make new friends at your new school. Doesn't that sound nice?"

"No. It doesn't!" Olive yelled
as she ran off to her room.
Lulu quickly followed.

"This is awful, Lulu. My dance recital is coming up and I was so looking forward to dressing up in my princess costume with all the other girls in my class!" Lulu climbed up onto the bed and laid her head on Olive's lap.

In her own way, Lulu was trying to comfort her pal. Olive's family got Lulu when she was just a puppy and the two had been inseparable since the day they brought Lulu home. They were each other's best friends.

The next day at school, Olive told her classmates that she would not be finishing the school year with them. It broke her heart to have to tell her teacher and friends she would be moving very far away.

Olive was so sad.
in fact, she cried the
entire bus ride home.

When she arrived home, Lulu was waiting for her as always and her mother had dinner cooking on the stove.

"Hi honey! How was school?" her mother asked cheerfully. But Olive walked right into her room, ignoring her mother's question.

She plopped onto the bed and closed
her eyes, with tears still streaming
down her face. Before she knew it, she
had fallen fast asleep.

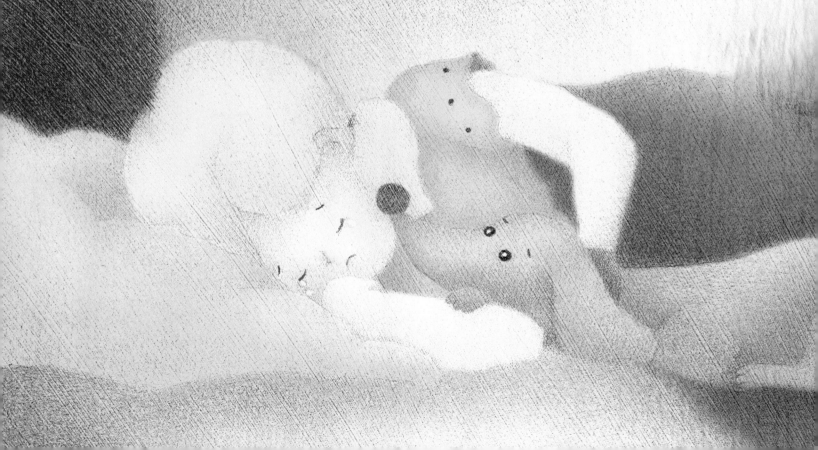

Suddenly, Olive found herself in a faraway
forest with no one else around besides her
good old pal Lulu, who, to Olive's surprise
was standing on two feet!

"Where are we?" Lulu asked. Olive turned
in disbelief. "Lulu! You can talk?"

"Come on," Lulu said, "I think I see something just beyond those trees way over there."

Olive saw something
too and cried out,
"There's my bed! And
my dolls, and look, Lulu,
I see your toys too!"

Lulu and Olive ran through the
forest toward these familiar things
unafraid of what might come.

Zooming past tree after tree, the two felt like they were flying—as if nothing could stand in their way.

When they finally arrived, they realized that
what had appeared to be their stuff was actually
a big scary monster with sharp claws and
scary-looking teeth. "Lulu! Run!" shouted Olive.

The friends sped off but, try
as they might, could not
compete with the monster's
slow but gigantic steps.

After running for what felt like forever, they came across a stick that looked like a sword. "Quick! Pick it up, Lulu!" Olive called out. "This will keep us safe."

As Lulu and Olive tried to catch their breath, the creature caught up and towered over them. "You'll never defeat us!" yelled Lulu pointing her sword-shaped stick upward at the beast.

But to their surprise, the monster hadn't been chasing them afterall.

In fact, he slowly walked over to Olive and her dog pal, picked them up, and embraced them with the world's warmest hug.

It became clear that he was chasing the two friends, but not with the intention of harming them. He wasn't something scary after all, just a really ginormous new friend.

He gave them both a
reassuring smile, so
delighted with the
friends he had just made.

"Oh no, my mom and dad are probably
wondering where I am," not realizing
they were in a dream.
"Lulu, we better go!"
"Goodbye, big guy!" Olive and Lulu
chimed in together as they ran along
their path in the forest.

Before she knew it, Olive was back
in her own room with Lulu sleeping
on the foot of her bed. "How
strange," she said to herself,
"I must have fallen asleep."

It was then Olive realized that what may look big and scary might be nothing other than a chance for something new and different. Even a new friend.

"Hmm," she thought, "maybe moving to a new place isn't such a terrible thing after all and change doesn't have to be scary. As long as I have my doggie, I won't have to face anything alone."

Olive walked into the kitchen, as sure as she could be.

"Mommy, I'm sorry I got so mad at you and Dad before. I am going to make the best of moving away and I'm okay with going to a new school and making new friends," Olive said with a grin on her face.

"In fact, I'm not scared at all!"

Her mother, filled
with relief and joy,
looked down at her
daughter and smiled.

The next morning, Olive's mother and father were just about finished packing up the truck with all of their belongings and furniture. "Olive!" Her father called. "Are you ready to go, sweetheart?"

Olive was sad to leave her classmates and her home but, with newfound confidence, she was ready for a fresh start in a new place with new friends and teachers.

As the family drove away, Olive's mother turned around to ask Olive something she'd been wondering about. "So what made you change your mind about us moving, honey?"

And Olive simply looked over at her old pal Lulu and smiled.

Kelly was born and raised in the San Francisco Bay Area. *A Tail of Two Friends* is her very first publication. In 2013, she received her Bachelor's of Arts Degree in Psychology with a Minor Degree in Counseling from San Francisco State University. Kelly works full time in San Francisco's vibrant tech scene and hopes that you find joy through her books.

Alexandria Gold grew up in Portland, Oregon where rainy days inspired a love of creativity. Today, her work is represented by the Bradford Literary Agency and everyday is an opportunity to be creative while working as an illustrator and crochet artist in San Francisco.

A special thank you my loving family & friends for your unwavering support, to Carol for the wonderful editing, to Franco for the brilliant inspiration, to David for all of your hard work making the website come to life, and of course, to my incredible illustrator, Alexandria!